D1083132

About the Book

The forest was bustling. Everyone was getting ready for the Autumn Bake-Off...a contest to see who could make the most delicious dish. Anyone could enter. Anyone might win!

On the morning of the Bake-Off, Mrs. Beaver looked over her list of ingredients. She was sure her gooey chocolate cake would win again this year. Meanwhile, Mr. Hare sat at his kitchen table and wondered what he should make. His spinach casserole and turnip soup had not gone over well. . . .

Mr. Hare's solution will delight readers, and it humorously proves that what is good for you can taste good!

THE BAKE-OFF.

by Lorinda Bryan Cauley

(A SEE AND READ STORYBOOK)

G.P. Putnam's Sons · New York

Copyright © 1978 by Lorinda Bryan Cauley
All rights reserved. Published simultaneously in
Canada by Longman Canada Limited, Toronto.
PRINTED IN THE UNITED STATES OF AMERICA
Library of Congress Cataloging in Publication Data
Cauley, Lorinda Bryan. The bake-off.
[A See and Read storybook]
[Food—Fiction]   I. Title
PZ7.C274gBak   [E]   77-24877
ISBN 0-399-61086-3 lib. bdg.

To Helen

It was autumn.

The forest was beginning to bustle
after a lazy summer.

All the animals were busy,
picking, canning and baking
for the long winter months ahead.

Soon it would be time
for the Autumn Bake-Off.
The Bake-Off had begun as a way
to fatten up for winter.
Now it was a contest to see
who could make the most delicious dish.
Anyone could enter. Anyone might win.

On the morning of the Bake-Off
Mrs. Beaver checked her secret recipe.
"Butter, sugar, flour, eggs . . ."
she mumbled, running her plump paws
down the list.

"My chocolate cake is sure
to win again this year,"
she said smugly.

Outside, Little Beaver and Little Hare
were playing hopscotch.

"You always win," shouted Little Beaver.

"But I bet my mom wins the Bake-Off today."

"My dad is a great cook too,"
boasted Little Hare.

"Sure if you like peas and carrots, yeck!"
Little Beaver shouted as he ran home.
"They make you big and strong,"
yelled Little Hare after him.
"Who cares!" Little Beaver shouted back.

Meanwhile in a cottage in the thicket
Mr. Hare sat at his kitchen table.
He stared outside at the garden.
The corn had grown tall,
the squash was ripe,
and the tomatoes were red and juicy.

"How can you beat a gooey chocolate cake?"
he asked himself.
Just then there was a knock at the door.

It was his friend Mr. Marmot.

"Good morning, Mr. Hare," he said.

"What are you making for the Bake-Off this year?"

"I'm still deciding," Hare answered.

"Not one of your nutritious recipes again, I hope," groaned Marmot.

"They just don't compare to Mrs. Beaver's delicious chocolate cake."

Mr. Hare thought about his turnip soup.
He remembered his spinach casserole.
There was always so much left over.
The young ones wouldn't even try them.

"Say what you will," Mr. Hare said. "Sweet desserts may taste yummy, but other foods like vegetables are good too. After all, you are what you eat."

"That may be true, but I'd rather win," said Marmot. "Well, I must be going now. I still have to make my sugar cookies."

"Vegetables *do* taste good,"
Mr. Hare said to himself.
He read over his recipes again and again.
He crossed out ingredients
and added new ones.
He even tried combining recipes.
Then all at once he had an idea.

"Okay, I'll play *their* game,"
he said with a chuckle
and he went into his garden
and gathered the ingredients.

Back in the kitchen

he sang a little song as he worked.

Late in the afternoon

the animals went to the pine grove.

It would soon be time for the judging.

The food was placed on long tables.

There were ooh's and aah's

as each dish was set down.

Mrs. Squirrel brought a rich walnut pie.

Miss Mink carried over a salmon mousse.

Bear showed up with a sticky honey pastry.
Grandmother Gopher brought along
her famous raspberry preserves.
Woodrat, the chef, had baked
a cheese soufflé.

Mr. Hare put his entry
next to the chocolate cake.
"I see you finally gave in,"
said Mrs. Beaver, eyeing his cake.
"Anything that is good for you
just can't *taste* good."

Hare shrugged his shoulders.

He sat down on a rock to watch the judging.

He smiled as he thought about

his secret ingredient.

The judges arrived.

First came Mrs. Fox,

the Home Economics teacher.

Next was Mr. Marten, a smart newcomer to the forest.

Last was Mr. Muscrat, who just plain loved to eat.

They began tasting at one end
of the table.
Everyone watched and waited.

Mrs. Fox chewed each bite daintily.

Mr. Marten's nose quivered

with each new, yummy smell.

Mr. Muscrat went back for seconds.

They sniffed and nibbled,
whispered and scribbled.
Finally they had it
narrowed down to two cakes.

"The chocolate cake is quite delicious,"
said Mrs. Fox. "But this other one
is even better."

"Yes, I must agree," Mr. Marten said.

"It is the best cake I have ever eaten.

Simply superb."

Mr. Muscrat had his mouth full.

He nodded and took another chunk.

Mrs. Beaver looked puzzled.
"But what is it?" she asked Mr. Hare.
"I thought I knew every kind
of cake there could be."

Just then Mrs. Fox made her announcement.

"The winner is," she said,

"Mr. Hare for his CARROT CAKE."

"Carrot cake?" everyone murmured.
"A cake made from a vegetable?
Absurd!" cried Mrs. Beaver.
"I don't believe it. I must
taste it myself."
She cut a small slice and looked
at it with a scowl.
Closing her eyes, she took a bite.
Everyone waited.

Little Hare glanced at
Little Beaver and grinned.
"Well," Mrs. Squirrel asked,
"How is it?"

Mrs. Beaver swallowed and paused.
"Simply delicious!" she said,
cutting herself another piece.

"Mr. Hare, I must admit
you won fair and square.
I must have the recipe."

"Why, certainly." Mr. Hare smiled
and took the last piece himself.

Mr. Hare's Carrot Cake

Cream

1   cup oil
1¼ cups honey
3   eggs (extra large)

Sift

2½ cups whole wheat flour
½   cup wheat germ
1   tablespoon baking powder
2   teaspoons cinnamon
1   teaspoon nutmeg
½   teaspoon salt

Add 2 cups grated carrots to creamed mixture. Then add dry sifted mixture and mix well.

Add 1 cup chopped walnuts (or pecans) and 1 cup raisins.

Bake in a 10″ tube pan, oiled and floured, at 350° for 1 hour or until done.

Frosting (optional)

Blend an 8 ounce package of softened cream cheese with honey to taste (¼ to ⅓ cup). Blend by hand or with a mixer and spread on top of the cake.

About the Author

Lorinda Bryan Cauley has combined her talents of story-telling, illustrating and cooking to bring us this delightful storybook.

She is a graduate of the Rhode Island School of Design and lives in Columbus, Ohio. She has also written and illustrated *Pease-Porridge Hot: A Mother Goose Cookbook.*